CHASES A PIZZA

Praise for the STICK DOG series

STICK DOG

CHASES A PIZZA

By Tom Watson

HARPER
An Imprint of HarperCollinsPublishers

For Jacob
(Y LIP TOM B NIT)

Library of Congress Control Number: 2014933033

ISBN 978-0-06-300688-1 (pbk.)

Typography by Tom Starace

20 21 22 23 24   PC/LSCH   10 9 8 7 6 5 4 3 2 1

❖

First paperback edition, 2021

TABLE OF CONTENTS

Chapter 1

A NEW OLYMPIC EVENT

Like many stories, this one starts with a search for something that ends up becoming a search for something else.

And it all begins like this:

Karen was chasing her tail.

Karen is the dachshund, as you no doubt remember. She loves to chase her tail. And Stick Dog, Mutt, Poo-Poo, and Stripes were all sitting around watching Karen

STRIPES

POO-POO

MUTT

KAREN

chase her tail. This is always good for some laughs.

You remember them all, right? Stripes is a Dalmatian. The poodle is named Poo-Poo. And Mutt is, you know, a mutt.

STICK DOG

And Stick Dog, of course, is our main character. My English teacher says I should call him the "protagonist" in my story because it sounds more professional and serious.

So, umm, he's our main character—and he got his name because I can't draw very well.

You know they're always looking for food. And you probably remember that the previous two books were all about the five dogs trying to get hamburgers and hot dogs, right?

Most important, do you know about our agreement? The one between you (the reader) and me (the writer and not-so-good illustrator)?

What's that? You forget our agreement?

Typical.

Okay, Mister or Missus Forgets-Everything-All-the-Time, I'll remind you. Our agreement is this:

I promise to do my best to tell you an engaging (hopefully funny) adventure story about Stick Dog and his four goofball friends. And you promise to not give me any trouble if my drawings aren't so good or if the story goes off in other directions now and then.

We have a deal then? Okay, let's get back to

Karen chasing her tail. Do you think she'll
catch it? I'll give you a hint.

Ready?

She doesn't.

It was especially funny to the other dogs when Karen got tired and laid her head down, curled her body up, and closed her eyes to rest for a minute. Then when she opened them, that tail was right there in front of her—just barely out of reach.

Oh, she had to have it. This time she'd get it for sure. And she lifted her chin off the ground and used her mighty four-inch dachshund legs to pounce after her own tail. And when she did, her body straightened out and—of course—her tail got out of reach again. And she started spinning around some more.

"Come on, Karen," Mutt said. "A little faster. Just a little faster!"

"Yeah," Stripes said, trying to suppress her

laughter. "You're almost there. Stretch out a little more. Just a little more."

"You almost got it last time," said Poo-Poo, his fur-covered belly panting in and out.

Stick Dog watched the scene with quiet bemusement. Oh, he enjoyed the fruitless efforts of Karen's tail chasing just like anybody would. But he also took great pleasure in watching Stripes, Poo-Poo, and Mutt as they watched Karen. This happens often with Stick Dog. He likes to watch his friends as they laugh because it makes him feel good.

Of course, Karen could only chase her tail for so long. Eventually, she had to stop. And when she did, this story really gets started.

"I have to stop," Karen panted, plopping down again on her belly with her chin on the ground.

"Too bad," said Stripes. "I really thought you were going to get it that time."

"Me too," said Mutt. He tried to hide a grin. "I mean, you seem to get closer and closer every day. Have you been working out?"

"No, not really."

"Well, it sure looks like it," Poo-Poo added. "Your speed has really improved, and I think you're bending and twisting better than ever before."

"You really think so?"

"Oh, yeah," Stripes confirmed. "It's totally true. If there is ever an Olympic event for chasing your tail and not catching it, you'll be a gold medalist!"

"That's so nice of you to say," Karen said, and began to push herself up from the ground. She smiled and nodded a bit as she regained some strength from this encouragement. "Thanks so much."

"Wouldn't you agree, Stick Dog?" Stripes asked. "Wouldn't you agree that if there was an Olympic event for chasing your tail but not catching it, then Karen would win a gold medal?"

Now, Stick Dog knew the other dogs were making fun of Karen. And, to be honest, Stick Dog was getting a kick out of the whole business. But he also knew when having fun was getting close to teasing. And Stick Dog didn't like teasing. So instead of answering, he turned to

Karen and asked, "What would you like
to do now?"

Stick Dog knew exactly what Karen was
going to say.

Chapter 2

MATH BY MUTT

Karen didn't hesitate. There was only one thing she liked more than chasing her tail. "Frisbee!" she yelped. "Frisbee. Frisbee! FRISBEE!!"

"Excellent idea," said Stick Dog. "Let's play Frisbee. And what are we going to need to do that?"

The other four dogs just looked at Stick Dog with blank expressions.

"What are we going to need?" he repeated.

Suddenly Mutt spoke up. "I know what we need! Our mouths! To catch the Frisbee with!"

"Well, that's true enough," said Stick Dog. "We definitely need our mouths. But I was thinking of something else. What is it that we catch with our mouths?"

This time Poo-Poo answered really fast.

He was so certain of the answer that he wanted to beat everyone in saying it. "I got it! Our tongues," he said quickly and proudly. And as if to prove his point, Poo-Poo opened his mouth and let his tongue drop out and began wagging it around. He snapped his mouth shut on it a couple of times by accident. You could tell it hurt, but he tried to not let it show.

Stick Dog didn't say anything for a moment.

"I guess you do sort of need your tongue a little to play Frisbee."

"See, see, see? I told you!" Poo-Poo said. His tongue flapped up and down and slapped his own face as he nodded with tremendous enthusiasm and vigor. "It's not easy being right all the time, let me tell you."

"Mm-hmm. I'm sure that's true," replied Stick Dog. "Now, who can tell me the most important thing we need to play Frisbee? Besides our mouths and tongues, I mean."

Mutt, Karen, Poo-Poo, and Stripes all turned their heads toward Stick Dog. Nobody said anything at all.

Stick Dog answered his own question. "We need a Frisbee."

As soon as he said it, his four friends all started nodding their heads up and down like crazy.

"Didn't I say that?" asked Mutt. "I'm pretty sure I did."

"It's so obvious," said Poo-Poo, "that I didn't think it was worth saying."

"I was going to say that," added Karen, "but Poo-Poo interrupted me."

Stripes said, "I was about to answer that exact thing. But the sun got in my eyes."

Stick Dog looked up at the sky. It was getting near dusk. The sun would be setting soon. He glanced at Stripes and shook his head. "Why would the sun getting . . . ," he began to ask, but then stopped himself. He didn't finish his question. "Well, I figured you all knew the answer. Let's find a Frisbee."

"That's easy," said Stripes. "You and Mutt were playing with one just a couple of days ago, Stick Dog. Don't you remember? It's orange. We found it by the basketball courts at Picasso Park. It's probably in the pipe by your sleeping cushion. I'll go get it."

"I don't think so," said Stick Dog.

"Why not?" asked Mutt.

"Think back," said Stick Dog, "to when you and I were playing Frisbee, Mutt. Do you remember what happened to it?"

"Oh, Stick Dog," said Mutt. "I can't remember that far back."

"But it was just the day before yesterday," said Stick Dog.

"That's what I mean," Mutt said. "That's a couple of weeks in human years."

This, frankly, caught Stick Dog by surprise. He asked, "What do you mean?"

"Well, dogs typically live about one-seventh as long as humans. So one dog day equals seven human days. The day before yesterday was two days ago to us—that equals fourteen human days. I can't remember that long ago," Mutt explained. "I always measure time that way. It's easier."

Stick Dog shook his head for a second and then asked, "It's easier for you to take a period of time, multiply it by seven, then pretend and think like a human to understand that period of time?"

MATH BY MUTT

"Yes, yes indeed," answered Mutt matter-of-factly. "And that is why I obviously cannot remember what happened the day before yesterday. It's the equivalent of fourteen human days. That's quite a ways back."

"No, it's not a ways back at all," said Stick Dog. He scrunched up his face and tried to understand what Mutt was saying. "It was the day before yesterday."

Mutt began to talk very slowly, hoping it would help Stick Dog understand. "It only . . . *seems* . . . like the day . . . before yesterday. It was really . . . two weeks ago."

"But that's only if you're measuring things in human-to-dog time," said Stick Dog.

Mutt nodded his head. "That's correct. I'm glad you finally understand." He was pretty sure talking slowly had really helped.

"But you're not a human," sighed Stick Dog. "You're a dog."

"Exactly."

Stick Dog stood there in front of Mutt
for a minute. He shook his head a final
time and turned to Poo-Poo, Stripes, and
Karen. "Do any of you understand this?"
he asked.

"We weren't listening," they all answered
in unison. To explain further, Karen added,
"There was a really cool-looking beetle on
the ground over here. It had a red stripe

running down its back. We were checking it out. According to Stripes, it doesn't taste very good though."

Stripes coughed a little bit.

Stick Dog turned back to Mutt. "Well, I remember what happened to the Frisbee the day before yesterday."

Mutt shook his head a little. "You mean two weeks ago. Do you want me to explain it again?"

"No, please don't," Stick Dog whispered. "Do you want to know what happened to it?"

"Yes, yes! What happened to it?" asked

Mutt, now greatly anticipating the answer.
He liked playing Frisbee just as much as
Karen and was looking forward to it.
"Where is it? I'll go get it!"

"You ate it," said Stick Dog flatly.

Mutt turned his head and lifted it just a little.
Then his eyes opened much wider, and you
could tell he now remembered eating the
orange Frisbee. "That's right. I did eat it."

TASTY FRISBEE

"You ate it?!" Poo-Poo, Stripes, and Karen asked all at one time.

Mutt looked down at the ground and pawed at the dirt a little. "I was hungry," he explained quietly.

Now, to you and me, being hungry is no excuse to eat a hard rubber Frisbee. But to all the dogs—even Stick Dog—this made perfectly good sense, and that was the end of this part of the conversation. Unfortunately, while that was the end of this part of the conversation, it did not solve the problem of playing Frisbee when they didn't have a Frisbee.

You all know what a Frisbee is, right? What with all these newfangled toys, gadgets, and who-zee-bangers, maybe you don't. Maybe we're too busy with our jet packs that fly us across the neighborhood and our particle-accelerator, atom-busting playthings to know what a Frisbee is.

Just in case you don't know, it's a flat
rubber disk that you toss back and forth
with a friend. And it's what the dogs need
to find.

"Let's spread out and find a Frisbee,"
said Stick Dog. "If we all run in different
directions, we're bound to find one soon
enough."

Mutt, Poo-Poo, Stripes, and Karen all
nodded their heads, agreeing that this was
a good idea on Stick Dog's part. When
Stick Dog ran off in his direction toward
Picasso Park, the other four dogs followed
immediately after him.

Has this ever happened to you? It happens
to dogs all the time. They know the

right thing to do and they understand the directions, but they just can't do it. They see a nice pair of headphones or a scrumptious-looking sneaker and they know they shouldn't chew the thing to bits, but they do it anyway.

But does it happen to *you*? You know the right thing to do, you know the proper instructions, but you just can't follow them? I think we all know the most common time this happens, don't we? Oh, you may not know what I'm talking about right this instant, but as soon as I say it you're going to know I'm right. Ready?

It's flossing your teeth.

We've all been to the dentist. And we've all

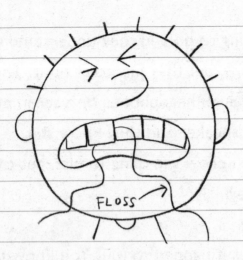

FLOSS

nodded our heads when the dentist asks,
"Are you going to floss your teeth every
day until your next visit?"

But do you? Come on now. Do you really?
Every single day?

If you do, good for you. You follow
instructions well, and you practice excellent
oral hygiene. And there are only about
seven of you in the entire world.

If you don't, join the club that consists of all the rest of us. Our club has nearly seven billion members. I mean, who wants to spend five minutes running a piece of waxy string between your teeth? Doesn't it make you feel like a fish caught on a hook? That's what I always think of. Now, brush often and don't eat twelve Reese's Cups for breakfast, I get that. But floss every day? Come on, I've got a life to lead, Cha-Cha.

Body hygiene, now that's a different story. I believe in being very clean and sweet smelling all the time. I live by one hard-and-fast rule: I shower once a month whether I need it or not.

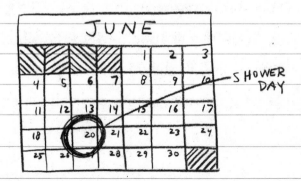

So the dogs didn't follow Stick Dog's instructions even though they'd agreed to do so. They simply tore after him to Picasso Park to look for a Frisbee. When they got there, Stick Dog turned around and asked, "Why are you all following me? We were supposed to run in different directions."

"I didn't hear you say that," said Stripes, looking away.

"I swerved a lot," said Poo-Poo. "So I went in a lot of directions but just ended up in the same place."

Mutt didn't say anything. But he did plop down on the ground and start scratching behind his left ear with his right rear leg. He kept almost tipping over and then catching himself at the last minute.

Karen said, "I actually ran in the exact opposite direction. Yeah, that's what I did. I circled the planet on the exact opposite path and—shazam!—here I am."

Stick Dog dropped his chin and raised his eyes toward Karen. "You're really, really fast."

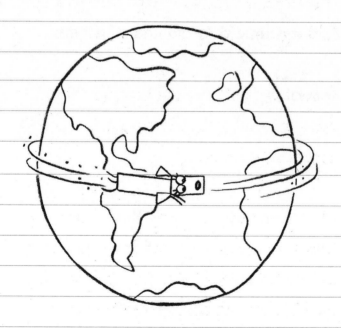

"Yes, it's true" was all Karen said.

"Well, we're all here now," said Stick Dog. "Let's find a Frisbee to play with. And this time, let's actually go in different directions to look. Meet back here in a few minutes."

This time they did follow Stick Dog's directions.

And this time they did find a Frisbee.

Sort of.

Chapter 3

THE FRISBEE SEARCH

So, yeah, the dogs ran all over the place to search for a Frisbee, and in no time, they were back. Stick Dog began to quiz the others and survey the results.

"I didn't have any luck," said Stick Dog. "How about you guys?"

"I found one!" exclaimed Poo-Poo. "It's rubbery and it's a circle and everything."

"That," said Stick Dog, looking at what Poo-Poo had, "is a bicycle tire. It's too big and flimsy and hollow in the middle. It won't glide in the air at all."

"Oh."

"Where'd you get it?"

"I chewed it off that metal thing over there," answered Poo-Poo as he pointed. "See that thing with the wheels and the handlebar and the cushy seat? I chewed it off that."

"That's a bicycle," sighed Stick Dog.

Poo-Poo looked at Stick Dog with a confused expression. "If it's a bicycle, why is that girl pushing it instead of riding it?"

Stick Dog closed his eyes momentarily and then opened them and answered, "It's missing a tire, Poo-Poo."

Poo-Poo looked over at the girl struggling to push her one-tired bike home from the park. "Jeez, that's too bad."

Stick Dog turned to Stripes. "Did you find a Frisbee, Stripes?"

"Yes, I did," mumbled Stripes.

"Great job. Where is it?"

Stripes began to look all around herself on the ground. She looked around her front paws, her back paws, and underneath her belly. "I know I have it here somewhere," she mumbled again.

Stick Dog said, "You're talking funny. Is there something in your mouth?"

Stripes's eyes popped open as if she just remembered something. She nodded. "It's the Frisbee!" she said, nearly inaudibly.

Stick Dog decided not to ask how an entire Frisbee could fit inside her mouth and simply said, "Let's see it."

Stripes lowered her head, opened her mouth, and sort of flung something toward Stick Dog. It clanked a bit when it hit the ground and then rolled up against Stick Dog's front left paw.

Stick Dog looked down at it but didn't look back up. "That's a bottle cap," he whispered.

Everyone was quiet and still for a moment. They didn't want to hurt Stripes's feelings, but it turned out her feelings weren't actually hurt that much at all.

"It may look like a bottle cap to you, Stick Dog," said Stripes defiantly. "But to a mouse, that so-called 'bottle cap' would make an excellent Frisbee. So if you really think about it, I did, in fact, find a Frisbee. You have to admit I'm right from a certain perspective."

"You mean from a mouse's perspective?"

"That's right."

Stick Dog stared at Stripes for a single second and then sighed, "Okay, Stripes. You're right from a certain perspective."

"Next time, please try to be more specific in your request," Stripes added.

"I'll do that," said Stick Dog, trying not to roll his eyes. He then turned to Mutt.

"Mutt, did you find anything?"

"Boy, did I! I was hoping you'd ask me next," said Mutt. He then did a most unusual thing. He spread out his legs, took a deep breath, and shook. There was a clunking, jingling, noisy racket as things fell out of Mutt's fur all about him. "I found a candy bar wrapper, an old pencil stub, a tennis ball that got hit and torn up by a lawn mower, a couple of good rocks, and

a piece of rope, and that's not even the best of it."

"Is the best of it a Frisbee?" asked Stick Dog.

"It's an old gray sock!" Mutt exclaimed. "I love these things! I'm going to keep it forever! I mean, you know, until I swallow it."

"But we were supposed to be looking for a Frisbee," said Stick Dog.

"Oh," Mutt replied, but he truly didn't seem to care. He was very, very excited about the dirty old sock. "I didn't find one of those."

At last, Stick Dog turned to Karen.

"I think I found just the thing," she said before Stick Dog could even ask. She dropped a flat cardboard circle in front of him.

"It's not exactly a Frisbee," said Stick Dog. He paced around the circle on the ground,

cocking his head a little bit and examining it. "But it is about the right size and shape. It just might work for a little Frisbee tossing. Good job, Karen."

"Thanks," said Karen proudly. "I really am quite excellent now that I come to think about it."

"Let's give it a try. Run out a little bit, Karen. We'll see if this thing flies," Stick Dog said, and picked up the cardboard disk in his mouth.

He bent his neck back and sideways, preparing to snap it forward, open his mouth, release the cardboard circle, and watch it fly.

Only here's the thing: He didn't. He kept that flat cardboard circle in his mouth. He remained in that paused, ready-to-throw position. Something peculiar was happening. Karen came running back. And Poo-Poo, Mutt, and Stripes all gathered around Stick Dog.

"What is it, Stick Dog?" asked Mutt.

"Are you hurt?" asked Stripes.

Thankfully, Stick Dog wasn't hurt. But he was surprised about something.

Very surprised.

Chapter 4

AN UNEXPECTED DISCOVERY

Stick Dog slowly straightened his body and dropped the cardboard circle to the ground. "You have to taste that thing," Stick Dog whispered. "I can't believe I'm saying this—but I think it tastes even better than hamburgers or frankfurters."

"That's impossible," muttered Karen, but she had learned a long time ago to trust Stick Dog when it came to the subject of food. They all began licking the cardboard.

Stripes lifted her head momentarily and asked, "What is this red, sticky stuff?"

"Here, let me see," said Poo-Poo, and he nudged his nose into a red splotch smeared across one section of the cardboard. He sniffed it, licked it, and then bit off a little piece and swirled it around in his mouth. He declared with great authority, "That red sticky stuff is delicious, no doubt. It has hints of salt and spice, and a fine, clean finish on the back of my palate. It evokes memories of tomato, green pepper, onion, and finely ground pepper."

For the first time, the dogs stopped licking the cardboard. They all looked at Poo-Poo with astonishment.

"What?" asked Poo-Poo. "You all know that I have very refined taste. That should come as no surprise."

Stick Dog said, "Well, Poo-Poo, it was a very fine description, I'll give you that. What about that yellow-and-orangish stuff on the cardboard near the center of the circle? What's that taste like?"

By this time, Poo-Poo had become even more caught up in his own expert tasting abilities. He leaned down and sniffed at the gooey blob in the middle of the circle. He licked it four times, nibbled off a little piece, rolled it around on his tongue, and then finally swallowed it. The others watched and waited for Poo-Poo's explanation of the taste.

"I must say," began Poo-Poo. "This wonderful goo is both extravagant and accessible. I'm reminded of my time as a puppy on the dairy farm, when the smell of milk and sweet cream would waft across the farmyard. It is, again, a slightly salty combination of flavors with a chewy, but not unpleasant, texture."

Stick Dog cocked his head a little. "I have to admit, Poo-Poo, you really have a talent for this sort of thing."

"Yes. Yes, I do," said Poo-Poo with a magnificent air of authority.

Describing food the way Poo-Poo does is a kick. You should try it at school sometime. When you're sitting in the cafeteria with your friends, pick up some weird thing on your tray and give a real fancy, snobbish description.

Let's use a Tater Tot as an example.

Do something like this: Stab that Tater Tot with your fork and hold it up in front of you. Then turn it around on your fork a couple of times. By doing this, you're going to get the

← TATER TOT

attention of the people around you.

Next, take a little nibble and cast your eyes up to the ceiling while you chew.

Then say something like this: "Ahh, Ireland. Home of the potato. What a lovely mixture of salt and starch. Breaking through the crispy outside texture to that soft, delicate potato goodness inside is both satisfying to my palate and pleasant to my stomach. It's perfectly balanced. And what a flavorful finish! I can still taste the oil that all six million Tater Tots were cooked in back in the kitchen."

Now, here's the important thing: When you're done with this kind of description, don't do or say anything else. Just get another bite to eat or take a sip of milk. The goal, obviously, is to freak out your friends.

With practice, you might even get as good as Poo-Poo. His descriptions of the flavors on that cardboard circle had instantly made playing Frisbee the last thing on anybody's mind.

And Stick Dog's stomach had begun to rumble. A sense of urgency had entered into the tone of his voice. "Karen, where did you find this cardboard circle?"

Karen nodded in a certain direction. "Over there. By the garbage can near the swings. It was inside a big, flat, square box."

"Box?" Stick Dog asked, and narrowed his

eyes. The other dogs had never seen him look so serious before. "What box?"

"I'll show you," Karen said, and raced toward the swing set with Stick Dog, Mutt, Poo-Poo, and Stripes in hot pursuit. When they got there, Karen showed them the flat, square box.

Without hesitation, Stick Dog read the
words on top of the box: "'Pizza Palace.

2207 North Clybourn Avenue.' Does
anybody know where that street is?"

"I know where it is," said Mutt quickly. "I
was hanging my head out of a mail truck
window once, and I saw it."

"Were you with your old human at the time? The mailman?" asked Karen.

"Gary? No," Mutt answered. He thought back for a minute. "It was so long ago, I can hardly remember. It seems weird, but I think I was being delivered or something. I climbed out of a box and saw an open window and just had to stick my head out of it. I love doing that. All the wind

blowing through my fur and the smells in the air. Yeah, I love riding in a car, man! That's the best."

"I'm sure riding in a car is excellent, Mutt," said Stick Dog, his stomach grumbling again. "In fact, you've told us about it before. And it sounds great. But right now, we're trying to find Clybourn Avenue so we can track down some more of these circles with the red paste and yellow-and-orange gooey stuff. Remember?"

"Right, right," said Mutt. He then nodded with his head over his left shoulder. "It's that way. Not too far. Just off Highway 16 before you get to the mall."

"Excellent. Let's go," said Stick Dog.

"Should we all go in different directions again, Stick Dog?" asked Karen.

"Umm, no," said Stick Dog slowly. "Not this time. This time we're all going to follow Mutt."

And that's exactly what they did. They ran out of Picasso Park and along the side of Highway 16 without ever getting close to the traffic. They knew better than that. They ran through grass and brush, and crossed a creek while running parallel to the highway. Soon they came upon a street with a small green sign at the intersection that read "Clybourn Avenue."

Chapter 5

DANDY DACHSHUND

"This is it," panted Mutt. "This is the sign I saw when I was hanging my head out of the window. Have I ever told you how totally awesome it is to do that?! Well, let me just tell you—"

"You've told us," Stick Dog interrupted, "in great detail. But right now, let's keep our minds on the mission. We have to find this Pizza Palace where they make these cardboard circles with the little spots of flavor on them. When we do, we'll search around the palace for some more of those circles and lick them all clean."

"I know what a palace looks like," said Karen. "Look for lots of pointy roofs and flags. And it should be made out of giant stones and be a really big building. It will also have a drawbridge and a moat with alligators. And I wouldn't be surprised if it's guarded by knights wearing armor and riding horses."

"How do you know so much about palaces?" asked Stick Dog.

"Oh, my mom used to tell me bedtime stories all about kingdoms and palaces when I was a pup."

"Isn't that nice?" said Stripes sincerely. "What a wonderful memory, growing up with your mom and all."

Karen smiled. "It really is a beautiful memory. It was a great six weeks."

"Okay," said Stick Dog, bringing everybody back to the mission at hand. "We're looking for the Pizza Palace. Keep an eye out for something that matches Karen's excellent description of a palace. And I don't know this for sure, but I believe the number '2207' has something to do with it."

"Maybe that's how many of these pizza cardboard circles they have there," suggested Mutt. "Wouldn't that be great?"

"That would be great," said Stick Dog. And all the stomachs of all the dogs began to grumble as they considered this possibility.

As they ran, the numbers on the doors were growing higher and higher, and Stick Dog knew that "2207" was significant. He had a good feeling that when they got to that number, they would see a great stone palace with flags and a drawbridge and a moat—and, hopefully, hundreds of tasty cardboard circles.

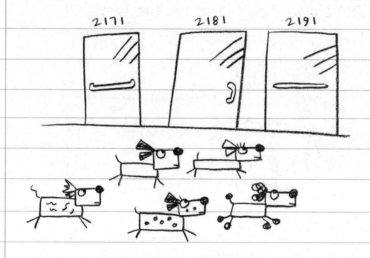

"Everyone, pay attention, please," said Stick Dog as he slowed his running to a walk and then stopped. Karen, Poo-Poo, Stripes, and Mutt stopped too. They positioned themselves in a circle around Stick Dog. "This is a good time to stop. We all need to catch our breath a bit."

"Good idea," said Stripes, who promptly fell over on her side. The other dogs, except for Stick Dog, did the same.

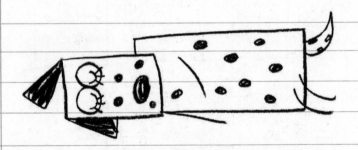

Stick Dog didn't mind. They had been running for some time, and the evening was growing dark. The first stars of the night began to sparkle overhead. "A little rest is a good idea. I think the palace is coming up real soon. We're going to need plenty of energy."

"How do you know we're getting close, Stick Dog?" asked Karen, not bothering to lift her head from the ground as she spoke.

"Well, the numbers on the doors of all these weird places keep getting bigger. We're already at '2135.' It was on that Starbucks store right back there. And we're trying to get to '2207.'"

"But we passed that Starbucks ages ago, Stick Dog," moaned Poo-Poo. He had gone from relaxation to total despair in a split second.

"Oh no. This is terrible!" cried Mutt. "We've been running in circles! We're never going to find the Pizza Palace!"

"I don't think we've been running in circles," said Stick Dog in a soothing and calm voice. He was pretty good at keeping his friends from worrying when it was unnecessary. "Clybourn Avenue is a straight line, and we've been running in the same direction."

Mutt lifted his head and nodded toward the Starbucks. "Then how do you explain seeing the same store again?"

"I think there are more than one of those stores," answered Stick Dog. "In fact, I think that's the fifth or sixth Starbucks we've seen on Clybourn Avenue."

"Of course, of course," said Karen, pushing herself up to her feet as if she had regained all her energy after this short respite. Now, let's be honest; for a dachshund to push herself up is not the greatest accomplishment. Their legs are, after all, only a few inches long. But Karen seemed proud of it all the same. She continued, "That makes perfectly good sense. You see, these stores sell stars—that's why they're called Starbucks. And there are literally dozens of stars in the universe. So they need many stores to sell them. I myself have seen more than twenty stars. Some of them are arranged in shapes even."

"What do you mean?" asked Poo-Poo. "Arranged in shapes?"

"Well, if you draw an imaginary line between certain stars, they draw a picture," answered Karen. She enjoyed when the others thought she was an expert on something. "There are lots of them. There's the Big Dipper, for instance. That's a famous one. It's up there somewhere."

"I see it!" exclaimed Poo-Poo.

"That's an airplane," said Stick Dog, but none of the other dogs paid attention to him. They were too busy listening to Karen. They had also perked up quite a bit.

"What are some other ones?" asked Stripes.

Karen was feeling even more full of herself now, and she began pacing around and lifting her nose to point every time she said a name. "Well, after the Big Dipper, there are many more. There's the Fire Hydrant. And over there is Tasty Biscuit. And, of course, who could forget Dirty Old Sock."

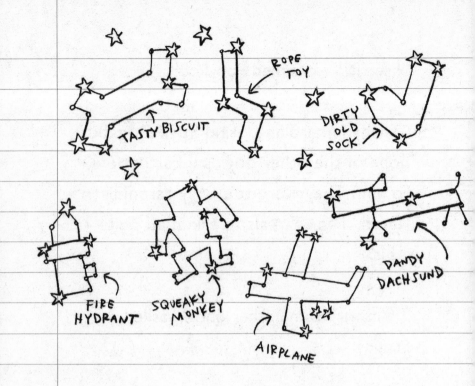

ROPE TOY

TASTY BISCUIT

DIRTY OLD SOCK

FIRE HYDRANT

SQUEAKY MONKEY

AIRPLANE

DANDY DACHSUND

"I love that one," said Mutt, jumping to his feet. "Where is it?"

"Over there, in the southwest," answered Karen.

"That's northeast," said Stick Dog. But again, nobody paid him any attention.

"Show us some more, Karen," said Poo-Poo, who had now risen from the ground and was searching the stars too.

"There's Rope Toy," continued Karen. "And, of course, Squeaky Monkey right under it. And my personal favorite is Dandy Dachshund. It's named after the ancient dachshund mythical hero. It's the brightest and most beautiful of them all."

"Tell us all about Dandy Dachshund, Karen," Mutt pleaded.

"Oh, there are so many stories," said Karen. "There was the time she defeated the Cats of the Acropolis. And the time when she showered all the dogs on all the earth with chewy bacon bits. And her epic battle with the evil warlord Hazel, who was trying to catch her with a big net and—"

A great grumbling sound interrupted Karen's list of Dandy Dachshund's epic achievements.

It was Stick Dog's stomach again. This made everyone remember how hungry they were. And their minds quickly turned from Dandy Dachshund's mythical achievements back to the delicious flavors they'd tasted

on that cardboard circle at Picasso Park.

"Everybody get a little rest?" asked Stick Dog. "Because I think we're getting close to the Pizza Palace."

"I know we are, Stick Dog. I know it!" said Poo-Poo, who was hopping up and down a little bit.

"How do you know?"

"Look right up there at that big, glowing sign!" exclaimed Poo-Poo. "Can you read what it says?"

"It says 'Burger King,'" answered Stick Dog.

"And where there are kings, there are bound to be palaces, right?!" screamed Poo-Poo.

Stick Dog thought about this for a moment. He nodded his head, squinted his eyes just a tad, and whispered, "Let's go."

Chapter 6

THE ULTRA-MISSIMO-PIZZA-SNATCH-O-METER

They passed the Burger King, a Starbucks, a flower shop, a camera store, a Thai food restaurant, a Starbucks, a Laundromat, and a toy store before they got to the storefront that had "2207" on it. And there in a big window, like a glorious beacon of hope and deliciousness, was a glowing neon sign that read "Pizza Palace."

"Where are the big, pointy rooftop

things?" asked Stripes from the little ditch where they had stopped to hide. It was slightly below the parking lot, so the dogs couldn't be seen.

"And the flags?" asked Mutt.

"And the moat with the alligators?

I really wanted to see them," sighed Karen, disappointment clearly in her voice. "I didn't want to see them too close, mind you."

"And the knights in armor?" asked Poo-Poo, turning to Stick Dog. The other dogs turned to face Stick Dog as well. They all had disappointment on their faces. "Do you think maybe they're down the street visiting the Burger King?"

He didn't have an answer. He was expecting all those things too. "I honestly don't know,"

said Stick Dog. He was staring at the front of the Pizza Palace, which looked like all the other stores they had passed—and not like a palace at all. Then the disappointment drained slowly from Stick Dog's face, and a slight smile began to take its place. "Who cares what it looks like? It doesn't matter at all. Don't you remember? I forgot a little bit too. We're not here to see flags and moats and knights and drawbridges. We're here to lick the heck out of those tasty circles! Let's find them, get them, and chow down!"

Well, this was exactly the kind of pep talk the other dogs needed. And in about one-half of one second, they started wagging their tails. They all shook a bit with nervous energy.

"I did really want to see alligators though," said Karen.

"I understand. I did too," said Stick Dog. He turned toward the front of the store. "Let's take a look through that front window. We'll see what's happening inside. That might give us a clue about what to do next. Poo-Poo, take a peek at the parking lot. Make sure there aren't any humans around."

Poo-Poo scooted up on his belly a couple of feet and then took a look over a guardrail to scan the parking lot. He then scooted backward in the exact same manner, getting his tail caught under his body a couple of times.

"What did you see?" asked Stick Dog.

"There are two humans in the Pizza Palace. A man and a girl," said Poo-Poo. "And there's one car and one truck in the parking lot."

"Did you say a car?!" asked Mutt. "Ooh, I love cars! Let me tell you, hanging your head out of a car is about the best thing I—"

"We know, Mutt," said Stick Dog quickly. "We know about the riding-in-the-car greatness. Let's keep our mind on the mission."

"Right, right," said Mutt. Then he whispered to himself, "Focus, Mutt. Focus."

"Anything else? Anything unusual?" Stick Dog asked Poo-Poo.

"No, nothing," said Poo-Poo. "Except the car has a sign on it that reads 'Pizza Palace—Delivery in 30 Minutes or It's Free.' I don't know what it means. Oh, and the truck says 'Big City Moving' on it."

"I've seen those types of cars before," said Karen. "I've seen them in the neighborhood. I chased one once for about seven seconds until it got away—*just barely*. The humans who drive them deliver those flat, square boxes. They

park the car in different driveways and then take the boxes to the doors of houses where the human owners come out and take the boxes inside. It's kind of strange behavior, to be honest. But it's definitely that type of car."

"That is strange, all right," said Stick Dog, and he thought about it for a moment. "It might be useful information later. Good spy work, Poo-Poo. And good info, Karen."

Poo-Poo bowed his head rather majestically toward Stick Dog. He said, "Thank you. Thank you very much." Then he bowed again for some reason.

Karen dropped down and scratched her belly on the ground.

"What do we do now?" asked Mutt.

"We need to survey the Pizza Palace to see what we're up against," explained Stick Dog. "The parking lot is clear of humans. So everybody follow me up to the Pizza Palace window. We'll take a quick look inside, gather some information, and run back here to make a plan. Got it?"

"Got it," Stripes, Mutt, and Karen all said at the same time.

"Don't worry, Stick Dog," Poo-Poo said. He held up his front right paw to stop everyone from moving. And he puffed out his chest. "We don't have to scout out the Pizza Palace. I know what we need to do. I already have the perfect plan."

"Really?" asked Stick Dog. "That's great. Let's hear it."

"Well, this whole idea of a palace got me thinking," began Poo-Poo. "And I think we should attack the Pizza Palace with something that's perfectly suited for such a thing."

"What's that, Poo-Poo?" asked Karen.

"A catapult," answered Poo-Poo. "See, we could have one of us operating the catapult. That'll be me. And the other four could climb one at a time into the ammunition-holding basket thing. That means I'll be able to launch four shots at the Pizza Palace. One of you is bound to go crashing through that big window. When

that happens,
the man and
the girl will be
so confused
and shocked
that we'll be
able to grab all
the pizza circle
things we want. Ta-da! Game over. No need
for any more plans. I figured it out. Any
questions?"

"Umm," said Stick Dog, and then he waited
a minute. "I have a couple of questions,
yes. First, where are you going to find a
catapult?"

Poo-Poo glanced away from Stick Dog.
It kind of looked like he was hoping he

would see a catapult shop at another strip mall down the street. "I haven't figured that part out yet," Poo-Poo finally said.

"Well, that's okay. No big deal," said Stick Dog. "Let's assume you get one. Don't you think that all of us—well, all of us except you—would get hurt from being used as ammunition? Flinging us over the parking lot and into that glass-and-brick building isn't going to be very good for our health."

"Hey," said Poo-Poo, "I just formulated a plan to get in there and get some food. I didn't know it had to be a plan to get us in there *safely* and get some food."

Stick Dog didn't say anything for quite a while.

Finally he did speak, saying, "I guess I should have mentioned that we needed a plan that doesn't hurl your four best friends through the air to smash into a building."

Poo-Poo smirked. "Umm, yeah. I guess you should have."

Stick Dog made one final comment to Poo-Poo about his plan. "When you find that catapult, let me know. And we'll certainly consider your idea."

Poo-Poo nodded in a businesslike manner. "Will do."

"In the meantime," added Stick Dog, "let's go look inside the Pizza Palace to see what's going on."

"That won't be necessary," interjected Karen before they even started moving.

"Why not?" Stick Dog asked.

"I have the perfect plan, that's why."

"You do?"

"Yes!" Karen exclaimed. She was getting really excited. "Do you want to hear it?!"

"Umm, sure," answered Stick Dog with a smidgen of hesitation in his voice.

Karen jumped at the opportunity. Literally. She was hopping up and down with excitement. "Okay! Okay! Okay!"

Even Stick Dog, hungry as he was, smiled at Karen's excitement. "What's your plan?"

"My plan is so excellent you might faint when you hear it. Really, you better sit down," Karen began. Stripes, Mutt, and Poo-Poo quickly sat down. Stick Dog remained standing as Karen continued, "It is a guaranteed success. We just need a couple of things to pull it off."

"What kinds of things?" Stick Dog asked. There was clear suspicion in his voice.

"Let's see, let's see," began Karen. "We're going to need a couple of rockets. Not too big, just medium size. And matches, of course, to light the rockets."

"Wait," said Stick Dog. But by now, Karen was on a roll. There was no stopping her. And Mutt, Poo-Poo, and Stripes were getting excited too. Their tails were wagging, and their bodies were trembling with energy. Nobody paid any attention to Stick Dog.

"We're going to need duct tape, for sure. And we're going to need at least two or three strong wrenches," Karen said. She was now pacing rapidly from side to side in the ditch. You could tell her mind was racing by how fast she was walking and talking. "We're definitely going to need balloons. I'm not sure how many, but at least a couple hundred. And they'll have to be blown up, of course. One bottle of ketchup and a jar of big dill pickles will be necessary. I'll need four tennis balls, seven balls of yarn, an empty backpack, and a sledgehammer."

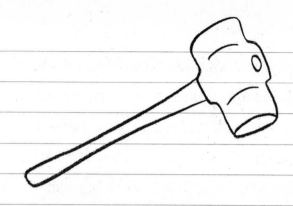

"Jeez, Karen," interrupted Mutt. Stick Dog was happy to hear this. He hoped that Mutt would be able to put an end to this nonsense. Then Mutt said, "It sure sounds like a great plan so far!"

"Oh, it is! My goodness, it is!" Karen exclaimed, and stopped pacing. She then tapped her front left paw against the ground quickly. "What else is there? Oh, right! We're going to need a stapler, thirteen pencils, and a bucket of warm water. Also, three dozen rubber bands. And, and, and . . ."

"And?" Mutt, Stripes, Poo-Poo, and Stick Dog all asked in unison.

"And a hairbrush, some tweezers, and a bowling pin." Karen let out a big sigh—big for a dachshund anyway. She stopped pacing but then quickly added, "Some chocolate chips, a garbage can, and a gallon of milk. Yep, that should do it."

Now, Stick Dog had heard a lot of crazy plans from his four friends before, but he had never heard anything like this. After all, this wasn't even a plan. It was just a list of things needed for a plan. "Karen," Stick Dog sighed. "We'll never find all that stuff."

"Are you sure?" Karen asked.

"I've never been so sure of anything in my life," said Stick Dog. "And even if we could get our paws on all those things, it would take weeks. I can't wait that long. I'm starving."

Karen nodded her head. "I understand, Stick Dog. But I sure wish we could."

"What was your plan going to be?" asked Poo-Poo.

"Well," answered Karen. "It wasn't really going to be a plan. It was going to be more of a thing."

"That sounds exciting!" Mutt said.

"It would have been," she sighed, dropping

her head a little in disappointment. "It was going to be a giant pizza-snatching machine. I had a name for it and everything. But it's not to be, I guess."

"What were you going to call it?" asked Mutt.

"I was going to call it the Ultra-Missimo-Pizza-Snatch-o-Meter, I think," sighed Karen. "That's just a working title, you understand. I might have come up with something better."

Stick Dog looked at her. "Karen, I have to tell you, I would have been really interested to see how that pizza-snatching machine worked. And I also have to tell you this: I love the name. I wouldn't change it a bit."

"Really?" Karen asked.

"Really."

"Thanks, Stick Dog. I feel better already."

Suddenly, though, Poo-Poo looked sad. He was hanging his head, and you could hear a soft little whine coming from the back of his throat. He was pawing at the ground just a bit and shaking his head sort of to himself.

"What is it, Poo-Poo?" asked Stick Dog. "It looks like something is bothering you."

Poo-Poo lifted his head to look at the others. "I wish I would have come up with a fantastic name for my plan like Karen, that's all. I really think the Ultra-

Missimo-Pizza-Snatch-o-Meter sounds cool."

Stick Dog didn't have time for this, but he didn't let it show. He just wanted to solve the problem as quickly as he could. "Well, Poo-Poo, your catapult shoots dogs into the air, right?"

"Right."

"Well, instead of 'catapult,' why don't you call it a 'dogapult'? In fact, why don't you call it the Super-Max-i-Matic Dog-a-Pult Pizza Bombard-o?"

It almost looked like tears were welling up in Poo-Poo's eyes. "I love it, Stick Dog," he whispered. "I absolutely love it. Thank you."

"No problem," Stick Dog said, and smiled.
He stretched his legs and said, "Come on,
let's go look in the Pizza Palace's window
to see what we're up against."

Chapter 7

RESCUE MISSION

They all began to climb out of the ditch to head to the Pizza Palace when Stripes said, "Wait a minute, you guys. Don't you think we should have a plan for the alligators?"

"What alligators?" asked Stick Dog. He could see the Pizza Palace clearly now that he was out of the ditch. It wasn't far away at all. He just wanted to get there and gather some information to make a plan. "What are you talking about?"

"Umm, in the moat," Stripes said as if this was really quite obvious.

"Oh, right," said Karen, nodding her head. "I forgot about the alligators. We really should have a plan for those things, Stick Dog. Stripes is right. They have sharp teeth and everything. Plus, I'm pretty sure that I'm quite delicious. I did catch my tail that one time, and it was pretty good. They're going to want to eat me for sure."

Stick Dog stared at Stripes and Karen for a moment. "There's no moat. Or alligators," he sighed. "Remember? We were all disappointed that there was no real palace. Just this store that looks like every other store."

"Right, right," said Stripes and Karen

together. Then, again in unison, they
asked, "What are we waiting for?"

And with that, they were off. With the
others following, Stick Dog climbed out
of the ditch, scooted under the guardrail,
sprinted past the car and the truck, and ran
across the parking lot—almost reaching the
sidewalk in front of the Pizza Palace.

Almost.

From behind him, Poo-Poo yelled, "Stop!"

All the dogs—including Stick Dog—
skidded to a halt. The nails on their
paws scratched and scraped against the
blacktop and spit loose pebbles clattering
all over the pavement.

Stick Dog turned to look back from
where he was—nearly to the sidewalk in
front of the Pizza Palace. Stripes, Karen,
and Mutt had raced past the moving truck
but were now stopped too. Poo-Poo
was at the truck—with his front paws
stretched up to the passenger-side door.

"What is it, Poo-Poo?" Stick Dog called,
attempting to keep his voice just low
enough to be heard. He didn't want to
draw the attention of whatever people
might be in the Pizza Palace. Stick Dog

whispered to himself, "Please don't be a squirrel."

It wasn't.

"What is it, Poo-Poo?" Stick Dog called again. "We're in kind of a hurry."

"We have an emergency back here," Poo-Poo said, never taking his eyes away from the truck's passenger-side window.

EMERGENCY?

"What kind of emergency?" Stick Dog asked. You could hear just a hint of doubtfulness in his voice. He began to step closer to the truck and—to his great regret—farther away from the Pizza Palace. He knew that this—whatever it was—would only delay their ability to gather information, formulate a plan, and then grab some delectable pizza circles to lick like crazy.

"A hostage emergency!" Poo-Poo answered quickly. There was a genuine sense of urgency in his tone.

"A hostage emergency?" Stick Dog asked as he got even closer to Poo-Poo. Stripes, Mutt, and Karen were listening to their conversation—and observing Stick Dog's actions.

"That's right."

"Where's the hostage?"

"There!" Poo-Poo exclaimed, and pointed at the window. "See? Those two paws?"

Stick Dog squinted his eyes, focusing as much as he could in the darkness of night. And he could indeed see two tiny, fuzzy paws at the very bottom of the window. "What is that?" he asked.

Poo-Poo finally turned away from the truck window for a few seconds. He stared directly—and intensely—into Stick Dog's eyes and said simply, "It's a kitty."

"A KITTY?!?" Karen, Stripes, and Mutt exclaimed loudly in unison behind them.

"Yes," Poo-Poo answered, and snapped his head back toward the window. "A kitty."

"Oh, for the love of—" Stripes said immediately, but then stopped herself. Then she whispered, "You can't be serious."

Karen and Mutt sprinted back to join Poo-Poo at the truck. When they got there, they looked pleadingly back over their shoulders at Stick Dog. They wanted to help the kitty too. That was really obvious.

It became instantly clear to Stick Dog that his friends were divided. Poo-Poo, Mutt, and Karen wanted to save the kitten. Stripes definitely did not.

Now, Stick Dog himself was torn between many, many things. And he knew the others were depending on him to make a decision. His stomach was grumbling terribly. He was so, so hungry. And being close to the Pizza Palace—and close to those cardboard circles with the splotches of flavor on them—only made him hungrier. But he also knew that if someone was in trouble, then he wanted to help. But he was so hungry.

But he had to help.

But he was so hungry.

He had to help.

He was so hungry.

Had to help.

So hungry.

Help.

Hungry.

Stick Dog could now
see the two gray
paws stretching and
struggling to find a
grip.

"See?" Poo-Poo
said. "It's trying to
climb up to reach
that crack at the top
of the window. It wants to get out!"

"Are you sure that's what it's doing?" asked

Stick Dog. He wanted all the information he could gather before making a decision.

"Am I sure? Of course, I'm sure. I'm positive," Poo-Poo answered quickly and desperately. "Listen to that whining!"

"It's trying to get out," Karen added. "The poor thing."

"Just listen, Stick Dog," Mutt called. He seemed to be getting upset and emotional. "It's so sad and pathetic. That little guy is being held against his will. He wants his freedom!"

MEEE-OWW!

MEEE-OWWW!

Stick Dog tilted his head and listened. It was absolutely true: There was a sad, high-pitched, and pitiful mewing coming from inside the truck. The sound was escaping through the open window.

It was that sound that made up Stick Dog's mind. If someone was in trouble, then Stick Dog was going to help. It didn't matter who it was or how hungry he and his friends were.

"Okay, let's save—" Stick Dog said, turning to Stripes, Karen, and Mutt. But before he could get any more words out, Stripes interrupted him.

"Don't even say it, Stick Dog," she said. "We are not going to risk getting caught or run over by a car for a cat."

"It's not a cat," interjected Poo-Poo. "It's a kitten."

"Same difference," retorted Stripes. Then she asked, "How do you know it doesn't *want* to be in the truck?"

"Are you kidding?!" exclaimed Karen. "Can't you hear it whining?! It doesn't want to be in there. I think it's a hostage-type situation. It's been uh, uh, uh—"

"What?" asked Stripes. "It's been what?"

"Umm," Karen said, and paused for a second or two. Then her eyes flashed open as she thought of the word she wanted. She said, "It's been 'kit-napped!'"

"Kit-napped?" Stripes asked.

"Yes," Mutt added with pure conviction. "Karen's right. This poor little creature has been kit-napped."

"I think you mean 'kidnapped,'" Stick Dog said, but the others were too wrapped up in the situation to hear him.

Poo-Poo was now growing more and more convinced about this theory. "Yes. Kit-napped," he said. "This whole crisis is where that word comes from. There are evil humans who drive around in their big trucks capturing little kittens. They're kit-nappers."

It was very silent for a few moments—except for the kitten's continued mewing—as they digested this information. Stick Dog was trying to think of a way out of all this and a way to finally, finally get those pizza circles to lick. He looked back toward the Pizza Palace to ensure nobody was coming out.

It was Stripes who broke the silence.

She lowered her head and shook it slowly back and forth while staring at the pavement beneath her paws. "I swear," she whispered. "Sometimes I don't even know you guys."

"What do you mean, Stripes?" Karen asked.

Stripes waited a moment, gathered herself a bit, and then began to speak very quickly in a lower voice than usual. "We are dogs," she began. "Cats are our mortal enemies, our adversaries, our opponents in life."

"And squirrels," Poo-Poo interrupted.

"And mailmen," added Karen.

"And Phyllis, the raccoon," Mutt said, and began to scratch his back on one of the truck's tires.

"As I was saying," said Stripes in a way that made you think she didn't want to be interrupted anymore. "Cats are our natural enemies. In the entire fifty-three-year history of the world, they've always been our enemies. Why, to suddenly start rescuing cats willy-nilly all over the place will turn everything upside down."

"What do you mean, Stripes?" Karen asked.

"It's just so unnatural, that's what I mean. It will upset the natural order and balance of everything," Stripes answered, and then tried to explain further with some examples. "The sun will start rising in the north instead of the south. The number four will come after the number seven—instead of after the number two like it does now. Red and blue will make yellow instead of orange."

"I never thought about all those consequences before," Karen said sincerely. Mutt and Poo-Poo nodded along with this sentiment. It seemed as if they might be changing their minds about the whole rescue-the-kitty idea. But they certainly didn't seem fully convinced. After a moment of careful thought, Poo-Poo seemed to switch back to their original position when he said, "I still think we ought to do it anyway. What do I care where the sun comes up?"

Mutt and Karen nodded along with

Poo-Poo. They had reconsidered their reconsideration too.

Stick Dog couldn't stand it any longer. They had to rescue this kitty and get to the pizza circles. He was just about to convince Stripes to join them all in rescuing the kitten. He opened his mouth to speak.

But he didn't have to.

Do you know why?

I'll tell you.

It was at that precise moment that the kitten inside the Big City Moving truck found its footing, clawed its way up to the window, and stretched himself fully upright against the glass.

It was then that Stripes—natural enemy to all cats and kittens all over the world— said a most profound thing.

Chapter 8

A TRIANGULAR-SHAPED CASTLE

"That's the cutest little thing I've ever seen!" Stripes exclaimed after taking one look at the kitten through the window. She came bounding toward the truck to see him even closer. "We have to save it! We just have to!"

Stick Dog, Karen, Mutt, and Poo-Poo all looked at Stripes—who was now waving and making funny faces at the kitten

through the glass. She was apparently
trying to brighten the little creature's
mood.

"But, Stripes," Stick Dog said. "Cats are
our natural enemies. You said so yourself.
We can't save the kitty, can we?"

Stripes had a very simple and succinct
response.

"Never mind what I said," she answered. She was now shaking her head and wagging her tongue loosely from side to side, attempting to get the kitten's attention. "I didn't know it was so totally cute!"

With that, the rescue attempt was on.

"Time to stack up," Poo-Poo suggested. "Just like when we were after those frankfurters. Let's do that again."

And at this suggestion—and without any further consideration at all—Mutt, Stripes, Poo-Poo, and Karen began bumping into each other, climbing on top of one another, and tumbling off each other.

Stick Dog stopped them as quickly as he could. He remembered how hard it had been—and how much time it had taken—back on that glorious frankfurter day. Ultimately, it had worked—they did get the frankfurters . . . just not quite in the way they had intended.

"Hold it, you guys," he said.

Immediately, the others halted their actions, placed all their paws on the pavement, and squared up to face Stick Dog. They could tell by the confidence in his voice that he knew what to do.

"We don't need to stack up as high as we did on that day," explained Stick Dog. "The top of that sheet on the clothesline was way higher than this truck's window."

Everybody was listening closely except  Stripes. She was flapping her arms like a chicken and jutting her head forward and back to try to get the kitten's attention. The kitten did not seem to notice.

"We're going to make a pyramid," Stick Dog instructed. "Mutt, Stripes, and Poo-Poo on the bottom. Me in the middle. And Karen on the top to reach the kitten."

"A pyramid?!" Karen asked. It looked like she was appalled at the suggestion. "Stick Dog, I'm afraid you have your historical periods all mixed up. We're at the Pizza Palace—you know: castles, kings and queens, that kind of thing. Not pyramids! Pyramids were around during caveman times. The cavemen would climb to the top of the pyramids to get away from the dinosaurs and Viking ships."

Stick Dog looked up at the sky and stared at the stars. He breathed deeply for several seconds. Then he said, "Thanks,

Karen. Thanks for correcting me with your historical accuracy."

"Happy to help."

Stick Dog then immediately said, "We're not going to build a pyramid. Instead, we're going to build a triangular-shaped castle. Mutt, Stripes, and Poo-Poo on the bottom. Me in the middle. And Karen on the top to reach the kitten."

"Great idea," Karen said. "Much better."

After the bottom three dogs were in position, Poo-Poo asked, "Are we going to have to share those cardboard pizza circles with the kitten?"

"Of course," answered Stick Dog. "We always share the food we find with the whole group. The kitten will be part of the group."

"Hmm," Poo-Poo said. "I'd like to reconsider this entire rescue operation then."

"Too late," said Stick Dog. "Brace yourselves—I'm climbing up."

And that's just what Stick Dog did.

And when he was stable atop Poo-Poo,
Stripes, and Mutt, he said, "Okay, Karen.
Come on up."

As Karen began to climb up, Stick Dog
stretched his neck higher to look at the
kitten through the window. During all
the commotion of getting stacked up, he
hadn't noticed that the kitten had stopped
mewing and whining. He hoped it hadn't
left the window.

It hadn't.

It was still standing there, arms outstretched and paws pressed against the window glass.

Stick Dog could feel Karen climbing up.

"Hold on a second, Karen," he said.

Stick Dog looked at the kitten's face. It didn't look scared at all. It was no longer panicked or whining.

It was smiling.

But it wasn't smiling at Stick Dog. It was sort of smiling past him. Stick Dog turned his head over his shoulder. Karen was still waiting to come up. Stick Dog wanted to see and understand what made the kitten

suddenly happy. When he looked back at the Pizza Palace, Stick Dog instantly understood what was happening.

There was a big human with a long neck about to exit the Pizza Palace. Stick Dog could see him through the glass door holding two square, cardboard boxes. He was pushing the door open with his right knee.

Stick Dog whipped his head around and looked at the kitten once more. Its smile was even wider.

Stick Dog said only four words.

And he said them fast.

"Run for the ditch!"

Chapter 9

SOUL MATES

There was no hesitation when the others heard the urgency in Stick Dog's voice. Karen jumped down and sprinted toward the ditch. Poo-Poo, Mutt, and Stripes ran as fast as they could too. Unfortunately for Stick Dog, this meant that his paws were no longer standing on anything, and he tumbled and fell. His left side smashed against the blacktop, but he got up

immediately and dashed toward the ditch.

When he got there, Stick Dog looked over the edge. Mutt, Poo-Poo, Karen, and Stripes huddled together at the bottom. There was panic and fear on their faces. They didn't know what was going on.

"Shh," Stick Dog said, and held a paw to his lips. "Stay here."

From a safe distance, Stick Dog watched the man with the long neck walk out of the Pizza Palace with two of those flat, square boxes.

"Good luck in the big city, Goose!" a man with a poufy hat called from the doorway.

"Take care of that new kitty, Goose!" yelled the delivery girl.

The man, who was apparently named Goose because of his long neck, waved back as he got to the truck.

"What's going on, Stick Dog?" whispered Karen, who was now at his side. Poo-Poo, Mutt, and Stripes were watching too.

"Shh," Stick Dog said, and watched some more.

The man with the long neck opened the passenger-side door and placed the

cardboard boxes on the seat. Stick Dog
was surprised to see that the kitten did not
make a run for it but instead looked up
longingly at the man—and mewed a single
time.

The man smiled, scooped up the kitten,
and walked around the moving truck to the
driver's side. As he did, Stick Dog could
hear him talk in a soothing and loving voice
to the kitten.

"Did you think I wasn't
coming back?" he asked,
and stroked the kitten
along the spine. "I'm
sorry you had to wait
here by yourself, little
fellah. But I *had* to get

my favorite pizza one last time. Who knows when we will be back here?"

With that, the man put the kitten back in the moving truck, climbed in beside him, and started the engine.

"I can't believe it," Stick Dog said.

"What?" asked all the others.

"That kitten *wanted* to stay with the human," he explained. "It didn't want to be rescued. It just wanted its human to come back, that's all. That's why it was whining so much."

"I'm going to miss the little guy," Stripes said sincerely. "It was like we had a special connection."

"Aren't you the one who didn't want to rescue him in the first place?" asked Poo-Poo.

"Let's not live in the past," Stripes said nonchalantly. "Instead, let me relish the special bond created here in this unique moment. I want to remember every detail of my time with that little cutie."

Karen, Mutt, and Poo-Poo kept shifting

their heads back and forth, looking at Stripes and then at one another. They were trying to make some sense of what Stripes was saying. Ultimately, they all turned to Stick Dog for understanding.

But this time Stick Dog just shrugged. He looked up at the sky—at the stars and the moon—and held perfectly still. It was as if he was seeking some sense of calm or inner peace while he was waiting for something to finish.

"We were more than just friends," Stripes continued as they all listened in bewilderment. She was now speaking in a tone that was more like a sigh than anything. "It was more than family. It was like we were soul mates."

"Soul mates?" Poo-Poo asked.

"Soul mates," Stripes confirmed.

"You didn't even know his name," Karen said, still trying to understand what was going on.

"I gave him a name."

"You did?"

"I named him after Stick Dog," Stripes

said. "Because Stick Dog came up with the triangular-shaped-castle rescue plan."

"You can't call a kitten 'Stick Dog,'" Mutt said.

"I didn't name it *exactly* after Stick Dog."

"What's its name then?" Karen asked. She was genuinely curious now. "Stick Dog Junior? Stick Dog, the Second?"

"No, silly." Stripes smiled and then paused for dramatic tension. She liked that everyone was paying such close attention to her. "His name is Stick Cat."

Mutt, Karen, and Poo-Poo all began laughing and chortling at this new name.

Stick Dog did not, however. He lowered his head, looked Stripes in the eyes, and said simply, "Stripes, I consider that quite an honor."

It was then that Stripes turned and watched as the red taillights of the Big City Moving truck grew smaller and dimmer as it rolled away.

Stripes waved at it and called, "Good luck in the big city, Stick Cat! May you find freedom and joy in your new surroundings!

Be well, my sweet comrade and fuzzy soul mate!"

The drama—and the time it was taking— had become too much even for Stick Dog to endure. He hushed Karen, Poo-Poo, and Mutt, who were still giggling, and said to Stripes, "Let's go get those pizza circles."

As the red taillights faded to blackness, Stripes sighed, "It's just so sad to see him go."

Stick Dog came closer and lowered his voice a little. "I know, Stripes, I know," he said. "But there is one good thing that you might consider."

"What's that?"

"We won't have to share any of the pizza circles we find."

Stripes considered this for a moment and looked back down the street to confirm that the truck had indeed disappeared. And then her stomach rumbled. "You make a good point," she said. "What's our next step?"

Chapter 10

A REALLY STRONG ANT

"Does anybody remember where we were going before we discovered the kitten who didn't want to be rescued?" asked Stick Dog.

"Back to your pipe to lick the pizza circles?" asked Karen.

"We don't have them yet," sighed Stick Dog.

"To find swords and cannons and stuff to attack the palace with?" suggested Poo-Poo.

"It's not a real palace, remember?" Stick
Dog said. He lowered his head for a
moment and closed his eyes.

"Stick Dog, are you okay?" asked Mutt.
He was tilting his head and trying to get a
better look at Stick Dog's face. "You look
frustrated or something."

"I know what it is," said Stripes before
Stick Dog himself had a chance to answer.
She had stepped her way close to him
and continued in a soft and loving voice. It
was the kind of voice your grandma uses

when she forgets how old you are—when she thinks you're much younger. Stripes continued, "Poor old Stick Dog is missing that cute little kitty already. Aren't you, Stick Dog? Are you missing the fuzzy-wuzzy kitty? Is that what's bothering you?"

Stick Dog raised his head. His lips were squeezed tightly together. He took a deep inhale of night air, and his facial muscles seemed to relax a little.

"I'm just a little hungry is all," he whispered.

Stripes's voice remained the same when she said, "Are you sure you don't miss the cuddly-wuddly kitty cat?"

"I'm sure," Stick Dog answered immediately.

He turned his head and eyed the Pizza Palace. He realized again just how close they were to that delicious flavor. He just had to lick some more of those cardboard pizza circles. His face grew instantly more serious. There was a sparkle in his eyes, his jaw was firmly set, and there was a renewed seriousness in his voice. "We have to sneak up to the Pizza Palace window to see what we're up against. We need to gather any information that might be useful."

Mutt, Karen, Poo-Poo, and Stripes could sense the fresh energy and commitment in both Stick Dog's voice and stature. They nodded their heads in understanding.

Stick Dog saw this, nodded back, and said simply, "Let's go."

They raced across the parking lot, past the delivery car, and to the sidewalk in front of the Pizza Palace.

Stick Dog scanned the inside of the place as fast as he could, turning his head left and right for information. When he was done, back they all went. They ran from the windowsill and across the parking

lot, scooted under the guardrail, and slid down into the ditch.

"Okay," panted Stick Dog. "I got a pretty good look around. And I know you guys did too. Let's gather all our information and then make a plan to get those circles. Stripes, what did you see?"

"There were two people inside," Stripes said. "One man behind the counter with a funny-looking cloud over his head. And the delivery girl was sitting in a chair by the door. Stick Dog, why are there clouds inside?"

"I think that was something he was tossing up and down over his head," said Stick Dog. "Not a cloud. But that was a great job. Thanks for being so observant."

By this time, however, Stripes had started digging a little hole in the dirt.

Stick Dog turned to Mutt. "What did you see?"

"An ant carrying a big crumb," answered Mutt.

"Inside the Pizza Palace?"

"No, silly," chortled Mutt. "On the sidewalk right under the window. He was really strong! That crumb must have been four times his size! It was quite something, I must tell you."

Stick Dog didn't say anything for a

moment. "But did you see anything inside the pizza store, Mutt?"

"How could I?" asked Mutt. He smirked a little at Stick Dog and shook his head ever so slightly. "I was watching the ant."

"Okay, thanks for that excellent report, Mutt."

"No problem at all. Glad to help."

Stick Dog turned to Poo-Poo. "How about you, Poo-Poo? What did you see?"

"Not a darn thing!" he said quite proudly.

Stick Dog hesitated for three seconds, and then asked, "Why not?"

"My eyes weren't open, that's why. Isn't that wonderful?"

"What's so wonderful about it? You didn't gather any information for our mission."

"Yes, I did," said Poo-Poo. "I know that we're in the right spot. As soon as I got to the sidewalk, I closed my eyes and took in all those wonderful smells coming out of that place. The dairy farm, the green pepper, and tomato. Oh, it was just wonderful. It was like tasting that circle all over again."

"But we already knew we were in the right place. We saw the big sign and the number and everything. We don't need to know what it smells like."

But by this time, Poo-Poo had lifted his head and was taking long sniffs of the air. "I think I can still smell it," he whispered. "Mmm, tomato."

Stick Dog was thankful that Karen spoke next.

"I saw something that I think will be helpful, Stick Dog," she said.

"That's great. What did you see?"

"I saw Mutt watching the ant," she said. "He was really obsessed with that thing."

At hearing this, Mutt rejoined the conversation. "You should have seen it, Stick Dog. The crumb that little guy was carrying was huge! It was really incredible."

"I understand about the ant, Mutt," said Stick Dog. He was working very hard to keep his voice and demeanor calm. But, in truth, he had smelled some of those scents coming from the Pizza Palace too. And he was getting hungrier and hungrier by the minute. "Let's just try to concentrate—

just for a little while—on our goal here."

He turned to Poo-Poo, who was still
sniffing the air, and said, "Will you take
a quick look at the parking lot? To see
if anything's changed? And we'll start
formulating a plan."

Poo-Poo scampered up out of the ditch
to take a look. In just a few seconds, he
scooted back down into the ditch. "I
thought you should all know that the girl
from the Pizza Palace carried out two of
those square boxes. She got into the car
and drove off. If we come up with a plan
quickly, we won't have to deal with her."

Stick Dog snapped his head toward Poo-
Poo and then back to the others. "That's

really important information, Poo-Poo.
Nice work."

Poo-Poo then kind of lifted his eyebrows
and lowered them again. He raised his
shoulders slightly. "Hey, what do you
expect? I'm Poo-Poo," he said, and quickly
scurried back to his lookout position.

Stick Dog stared at where Poo-Poo had
been, not quite sure he had just heard
what he thought he heard. Then he
remembered his report and quickly turned
to Mutt and Stripes. "You heard what
Poo-Poo said. Now's the perfect time to
put a plan into action. Quickly! Do either
of you have a plan?"

They both did.

Chapter 11

TRIP-A-DOOS

"I have a plan," answered Mutt. "And while I admire Poo-Poo's Super-Max-i-Matic Dog-a-Pult Pizza Bombard-o and Karen's Ultra-Missimo-Pizza-Snatch-o-Meter from earlier, I think that you'll find my plan to be a little more practical."

"Sounds good," said Stick Dog.

"It involves the car that girl drove away in," Mutt began.

But Stick Dog stopped him right there.

"It doesn't involve driving the car, does it? We heard a plan like that back at Picasso Park when we were trying to get those hamburgers. And none of us knows how to drive."

"No, no. Don't be ridiculous," said Mutt, shaking his head and then turning serious. "See, what we do is hide around the corner of the Pizza Palace. And then we keep an eye out for that girl to come driving back from wherever she is, see. When she pulls into the parking lot, we all run out to different parking spaces. There are only about five spots in front of the pizza shop and there are five of us, so that works out perfectly. When she pulls in: Crunch! Yelp! Pizza!"

Stick Dog pulled his mouth to one side.
"I'm not sure I get it," he said slowly.
"What exactly is 'Crunch! Yelp! Pizza!'?"

You could tell Mutt was feeling pity for
Stick Dog. He took a few steps toward him
and sat down on his back legs next to him.
Then Mutt put one of his front legs around
Stick Dog's shoulder. "It's okay, Stick Dog. I
know you're real hungry, and maybe that's
affecting your brain functionality. Don't feel

bad about it. I'll go over it again. I'll try to use more simpler language."

"Umm, thanks. Go ahead."

"We hide around corner of shop," began Mutt slowly. "Girl drives car. Into parking lot. We each run to different parking space. Crunch! Yelp! Pizza!"

"Could you give me the details about the 'Crunch!' part?" asked Stick Dog.

"Of course, buddy," said Mutt as he looked into Stick Dog's eyes with great empathy and patted his paw a few times on Stick Dog's shoulder. "That's when one of us gets a leg run over by the car."

"That's what I thought," said Stick Dog. "And the 'Yelp!' part of the plan?"

"It's when one of us—"

"The one with crushed leg bones?" interrupted Stick Dog.

"That's right, old pal—the one with crushed leg bones," said Mutt, still patting Stick Dog on the shoulder. "That's when the one with the crushed leg bones begins to yelp and scream in anguish and pain."

"I figured," said Stick Dog. "And the 'Pizza!' part of the plan?"

"That's when the pizza man runs out to see what happened because of all the yelping. When he does, we run in and grab all the pizza circles we can find. It will be the feast of a lifetime!"

"Except for the one with the crushed leg," said Stick Dog. "That one will probably be in too much pain."

Mutt lowered his voice a little and spoke very softly. "That's right, buddy. Except for the one with the crushed leg."

"I understand fully now, Mutt," Stick Dog said. He also gently removed Mutt's paw from his shoulder. "Thanks for taking the time to explain your most excellent plan in full detail to me. I'm making an assumption here, but I bet your plan has a name, doesn't it?"

"It does, yes," Mutt said, and smiled a bit. "It's called the Break-a-Leg-and-Scream-in-Pain-for-Pizza-Circles Fantacular. It's a great name isn't it?"

"It is a great name, yes," said Stick Dog, nodding his head.

"And a great plan?"

Stick Dog didn't want to say it wasn't a great plan. He had, as you probably know by now, a nice way of saying something was bad without hurting anybody's feelings.

So Stick Dog said, "I think it's a very interesting plan, Mutt. It's logical, and I love how it involves everybody. By the way, who is it that gets their leg shattered by the car?"

"There's no way of knowing," answered Mutt. "It all depends on which parking spot that girl pulls into. It could be Poo-Poo, Stripes, or Karen. It could even be you, Stick Dog."

"I see," said Stick Dog. "And could it also be you?"

It was a very strange expression that came across Mutt's face just then. It was as if this idea had never occurred to him at all—and he really didn't like it. He pulled his head back a little and winced a bit in imaginary pain.

It took him a couple of seconds to gather himself, and then he said, "Stick Dog, I know it's a great plan and a great name and all that. But I'm thinking I shouldn't get to have all the glory and take all the credit when we end up licking those cardboard pizza circles. It just doesn't seem fair. In fact, I'm a little embarrassed just how superior my plan actually is. I would, therefore, like to withdraw my plan from consideration for the time being."

"Okay, Mutt," said Stick Dog. "I think that's a very kind and honorable thing to do."

"Well, as you know," said Mutt, "I'm all about honor."

"Yes, I know."

Poo-Poo darted back down into the ditch just then. He reported, "That girl is back with the car. She just went into the Pizza Palace again."

"Shoot. That's only going to make things harder," Stick Dog said sharply. "But it's good information to have."

"Happy to help."

"Can you let us know of any further developments?" Stick Dog asked Poo-Poo.

Poo-Poo didn't answer, but he did salute Stick Dog rather formally before returning to his lookout spot.

Stick Dog did not return the salute. Instead, he looked toward Stripes. "Let's hear your plan. Quickly."

"Well, it's dark, right?" Stripes started right away. You could tell that she was feeling pretty darn confident about her plan. She had a little grin on her face as she began to explain things.

"Right," Stick Dog answered slowly.

TRIP-A-DOO

"And trip-a-doos come out at night, of course," answered Stripes. "We just have to round up a bunch of trip-a-doos. About eight or ten of them should do the trick."

Now, this was a statement that nobody was expecting. And there was a very good reason for that: none of them had ever heard the word before. In fact, Stick Dog was fairly certain that "trip-a-doos" wasn't a word at all. He had to ask, "What are trip-a-doos?"

"Oh, they're these little shape-shifting creatures that usually come out when it's really dark outside."

"Shape-shifting?" asked Stick Dog.

"That's right. They can change shape," Stripes confirmed, and nodded. "They're funny little things actually. When you're walking or running at night, these trip-a-doos come out. Then they sneak right in front of you, and you trip over them. They get me at night all the time. I'm always falling all over the place at night because of trip-a-doos."

Stick Dog, who was now hungrier than ever, could not resist investigating this a little bit more. He was just too curious.

"What do they look like? These trip-a-doos?"

"That's where the shape-shifting comes in," explained Stripes. She was starting to look a little surprised that her friends appeared to be completely unfamiliar with trip-a-doos. "By the time you get up after smashing into the grass or the blacktop or whatever, those sneaky little buggers have shape-shifted into totally different things."

Stick Dog was working very hard not to smile. He couldn't even look at Mutt and Karen. He was sure they were both about to burst out laughing. He asked Stripes, "What kinds of things do they shape-shift into after they trip somebody?"

"Oh, just about anything," Stripes answered, and glanced toward the sky trying to remember. "A crack in the sidewalk, a hole in the road, a cardboard box. In the forest, they like to turn into logs a lot. And roots and vines and that kind of stuff."

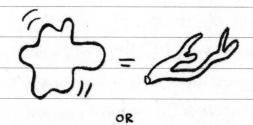

OR

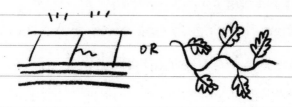

Stick Dog nodded. "Couldn't you just be tripping over those things themselves? You know, logs and sidewalk cracks and stuff?"

Stripes raised her eyebrows. "I would never trip over things like that. I'm far too graceful."

"I see."

"You know what?!" Mutt exclaimed. He seemed suddenly anxious to share something with the group. "Just last night I was leaving Stick Dog's pipe after I'd finished chewing up one of his extra tennis balls—I LOVE those things. I was walking through the woods and—Yank!—I caught my ankle on something and smashed face-first into the ground."

"What did you trip on?" Karen asked.

"Well, at first I thought it was a fallen tree branch—I could see it in the moonlight when I got up. But now I know better," Mutt explained. "Now I know it was one of those trip-a-doo creatures that changed into a tree branch right after I fell down."

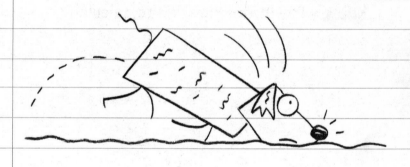

"That was a trip-a-doo, all right. That's exactly how they behave," Stripes said, and nodded her head in full understanding. "And that's what we're going to use to trip the pizza delivery girl when she walks out the door. We just need to go find a bunch of trip-a-doos."

"Well, I sure am glad to know about them," said Mutt. He was relieved.

Now, Stick Dog, quite honestly, didn't know what to do. He tried to calculate

what would work faster—and get them
to the pizza circles faster: disproving
the existence of trip-a-doos or coming
up with a way out of Stripes's plan that
utilized nonexistent trip-a-doos.

But he never had to make the decision.

That's because Poo-Poo came back from
his lookout spot right then. He had a very
important announcement.

Chapter 12

FRISBEE TIME

Poo-Poo was panting. The others could
see that he was excited.

"There's something going on, Stick

Dog," he said quickly. "The pizza man is stacking a whole bunch of those square boxes on the counter. There must be a dozen of them so far! The girl's just standing at the counter kind of waiting. Thought you should know."

Stick Dog listened very closely. One of his eyes was squinted nearly shut. His head was tilted. There was a single wrinkle across his forehead.

Then his eyes flashed open wide.

He had just figured something out— and the other dogs could tell instantly.

"What is it, Stick Dog?" Poo-Poo asked.

Mutt, Karen, and Stripes all came closer.
They could tell something important was
happening.

"The delivery girl is going to load the car!"
Stick Dog said urgently. "And when she
does, we'll be ready!"

"What about my trip-a-doos plan?"
asked Stripes. She was noticeably
disappointed.

"We'll have to use it another time," Stick
Dog answered as fast as he could. "It's a
wonderful strategy. We just don't have
time to track down a bunch of trip-a-doos
right now."

"Okay," Stripes said. She seemed satisfied enough.

"What are we going to do?" Mutt asked. "What's the plan?"

"I'll tell you exactly what we're going to do," answered Stick Dog. Poo-Poo, Stripes, Mutt, and Karen had rarely seen him look so completely focused, so absolutely determined, so completely sure of himself.

They knew the time had come. They were going to go get those cardboard pizza circles with the little blotches of flavor on them. They started moving with nervous energy. Karen was hopping up and down on her small but powerful dachshund legs. Mutt shook out his fur, trying to

increase his potential speed by losing
any unnecessary weight. Stripes started
loosening up by rolling her neck around
in a circle. And Poo-Poo bumped his head
face-first into the side of the ditch a couple
of times.

"That pizza girl is going to start carrying
some of those boxes to the car," Stick Dog
said. He was speaking very quickly and giving
rapid-fire instructions. "When she does, we
make our move. She's going to carry a stack
of boxes out and put them in the car. Then
she'll return to the store to get some more.
When she does, I'm going to sprint to the
car, grab a square box, and open it. I'll grab
a pizza circle out."

"Then what?" asked Karen.

"Then," answered Stick Dog with a smile, "we finally get to play some Frisbee."

"Ooh, I love Frisbee!" shouted Karen.

"I know you do," said Stick Dog. He continued with the plan very quickly. "We're going to form a Frisbee relay line across the parking lot. But we're going to use the cardboard circles for Frisbees. Stripes, you'll be next in line nearest me. I'll throw it to you, then you throw it to Mutt, who will be in the middle of the parking lot. Mutt, after you catch it from Stripes, you fling it to Poo-Poo, who will be over by the guardrail. And Poo-Poo tosses it to Karen at the top of the ditch. She'll drop them in from there. Then we'll repeat the whole process. We should be able to get a nice-sized pile of circles in no time."

By now, the four dogs were absolute bundles of energy, and Stick Dog could tell they were ready.

"Let's do this thing," he said.

With that, they scurried out of the ditch and stopped to stare over the guardrail at the edge of the parking lot. In just a minute, the pizza girl did exactly what Stick

Dog had anticipated: she carried a stack of five pizza boxes to the car. She balanced the stack on her knee as she opened the car door and set it inside on the backseat.

"Leave the door open, leave the door open," Stick Dog whispered. "Please leave the door open."

She did.

And Stick Dog smiled, turned to the other dogs, and said, "Let's go."

As soon as the pizza girl began walking back toward the Pizza Palace, things moved very fast. The dogs rushed to their positions, and Stick Dog sprinted to the car. He propped himself up on the

backseat, pulled up the lid of the square
box on the top of the stack, and then
made the most fantastic discovery of his
life.

What he found was not a cardboard pizza
circle with a few blotchy stains of flavor on
it. No, what he found was an entire

pizza sitting atop the cardboard circle inside that flat, square box. He could see the cardboard edge under the pizza's crust. He could smell the aromas of tomato sauce and mozzarella cheese, and luscious chewy crust—not too doughy, not too crispy. He felt the warmth rising up to meet him.

What they had found at Picasso Park, Stick Dog now realized, was simply the used cardboard with a few old crumbs and drips from a long-ago eaten pizza. What he was seeing and smelling now was a pizza itself. Freshly baked and ready to devour.

It was, perhaps, the most surprising and amazing discovery in the history of the world. Well, in Stick Dog's world, anyway.

He wanted to bite into it right then and there, but he knew he had no time—and there were four other dogs waiting for him to act and share the food. He couldn't let them down.

Most of all, he knew the pizza girl would be back at any minute with another stack of square boxes to put in the car.

Stick Dog gripped the pizza in his mouth,

slid it out of the box, and backed out of the
car. He pulled his head to the side, whipped
it forward, and opened his mouth. The
pizza glided gracefully through the air. It
was a thing of pure elegance as it flew. The
aerodynamics of the pizza were perfect as it

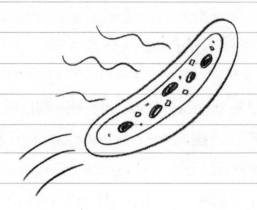

soared toward Stripes. She was there, about
a third of the way across the parking lot,
with her mouth open, waiting to make the
catch and fling it to Mutt.

That's right when the pizza landed on her head, slid down her neck and onto the ground.

Stick Dog watched for only a second as Stripes picked it up and flung it to Mutt. He knew he had no time and couldn't wait to watch the results of the pizza relay line. There were still four pizzas in the backseat.

Stick Dog climbed back into the car. In quick succession, he retrieved the second and third pizzas and flung them in Stripes's direction. He knew he had to look into the Pizza Palace to see if the girl was coming.

She was.

She was holding four boxes this time
and had almost stepped out through the
doorway.

Stick Dog had no
more time—he had
to go. He glanced
at the line of dogs
across the parking
lot. All of them had
a tangled, gooey
mess of tomato
sauce and cheese
covering some part
of their bodies.
Stripes had some
down her neck. Mutt
had some on his back. Poo-Poo was trying
to lick a big splotch of pizza on his side.

And Karen couldn't be seen at all. She was,
in fact, under a pizza right at the top of the
ditch. She was small enough to fit under it,
and Stick Dog could see the pizza moving up
and down as she struggled beneath it.

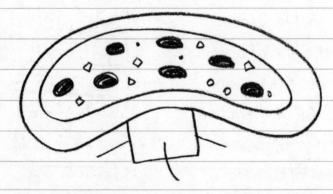

He instantly surmised that none of them
was a very good Frisbee thrower. And he
was even more certain that they were all
very bad Frisbee catchers.

But he had no choice. He had to leave.
They all had to leave and get back to the

ditch. The girl was at the door. Stick Dog took his first step away from the car when a wonderful sound came from the Pizza Palace.

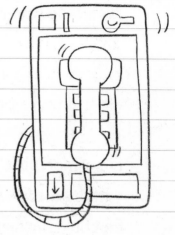

Do you know what it was?

It was the ringing of a telephone.

When that phone rang, the pizza girl pivoted at the door, turned, and went back into the Pizza Palace. There, she set the pizza boxes back down on the counter and walked out of view to answer the phone. Stick Dog could hear what she said when she picked up the phone.

"Hello! It's the Pizza Palace! Will this

be pickup or delivery?"

Stick Dog knew one thing. One miraculous thing.

He had more time.

He climbed back into the car and withdrew the fourth pizza as quickly as he could. Instead of flinging it to Stripes,

Stick Dog sprinted across the parking lot with the pizza in his mouth and dropped it neatly at the side of the ditch. Karen had made a little progress getting out from under the pizza that had landed on her. Her face was now sticking out a few inches from beneath the pizza.

"I'll be right back," he panted.

"I'll be here," said Karen. And then, with great enthusiasm, she added, "Run, Stick Dog, run!"

And that's exactly what he did. He got back to the car, snatched the fifth and final pizza, carried it across the lot, and dropped it neatly right next to the others.

By this time, Mutt, Poo-Poo, and Stripes were helping Karen escape from her pizza imprisonment. Stick Dog ran across the lot a final time, climbed into the car, and restacked the now-empty boxes in the backseat as quickly as he could. As he exited, he could hear the pizza girl ending her telephone conversation.

She said, "Right, got it. We'll be there in thirty minutes or less—guaranteed. Bye!"

The pizza man was beginning to toss more dough up in the air, and the girl came back

to the counter. By the time she made it
to the door with the stack of boxes again,
Stick Dog was already at the guardrail. And
by the time she started the car, he was in
the ditch with Karen, Poo-Poo, Mutt, and
Stripes.

They all had splotches of pizza stains
somewhere on them, but none of them
cared. There was one messy mound of
pizza that was piled up with pieces sticking
out here and there. It may not sound very

appetizing to you and me, but to the dogs it didn't make any difference. They usually liked to eat their food in piles, anyway.

And two pizzas were in perfect shape.

There were no words exchanged. The dogs simply began to eat and eat.

Finally, Karen took a break between bites and said, "This is even better than that cardboard circle!"

Stick Dog looked up and swallowed the bite he had in his mouth. And then he took a minute to watch his friends enjoy their meal.

And he smiled as he watched them eat.

The End

Tom Watson lives in Chicago with his wife, daughter, and son. He also has a dog, as you could probably guess. The dog is a Labrador-Newfoundland mix. Tom says he looks like a Labrador with a bad perm. He wanted to name the dog "Put Your Shirt On" (please don't ask why), but he was outvoted by his family. The dog's name is Shadow. Early in his career Tom worked in politics, including a stint as the chief speechwriter for the governor of Ohio. This experience helped him develop the unique storytelling narrative style of the Stick Dog, Stick Cat, and Trouble at Table 5 books. Tom's time in politics also made him realize a very important thing: kids are way smarter than adults. And it's a lot more fun and rewarding to write stories for them than to write speeches for grown-ups.

Visit www.stickdogbooks.com for more fun stuff.

Also available as an ebook.